# Hullabaloo on Main Street

*Lela Markham*

Published by Breakwater Harbor Books

"Hullabaloo on Main Street" is a work of fiction and meant to be satirical. Any resemblance to yourself or people you know is completely coincidental.

# A Word from Lela Markham

The 21st century political landscape has not been easy on the American people. It has opened big divides between us ... divides that have existed for a long time, but were surmountable when we were will to talk about them and find solutions that might not please everyone all the time, but didn't leave half of us feeling left out in the cold.

Those days are gone and starting with the election of George W. Bush in 2000, some of us are no longer willing to accespt the outcome of the republican democratic process. We aver we are committed democrats until the election doesn't go our way, then we vow a revolution in the streets to change the results.

I'm not blaming anyone. I'm just stating a fact.

When I read about a Wisconsin rural community where half of the population was devastated that the other half voted for Donald Trump instead of their preferred candidate, Hullabaloo on Main Street was born. I hope it makes you laugh as much as it makes you think, because the character of Connor inhabits a different thought process that stands outside of the right-left, red-blue, conservative-progressive, Republican-Democrat dichomy that characterizes America's political discussions today. There are actually more than two sides to the issues. Connor doesn't exactly agree with either side, but he's not a moderate either. And from that refreshing perspective, he offers a solution to our current battle of the bubbles.

Hope you enjoy it!

# Thanks!

The people who inadvertently helped me to write this novelette shall mostly remain nameless. There were Democrats and Republicans, progressives and conservatives who contributed many little nuggets of humor without knowing it. I think they would probably prefer to entertain us from the shadows and I prefer to keep their friendships.

Josh Bennett and Michael Anderson from Patriot's Lament radio show (KFAR AM 660) provided a basic template for Connor, my libertarian anarchist who bravely enters both bubbles on Election Wednesday. Like a lot of my characters, he took over from there.

To my husband for being a beta reader on this short work of fiction. It's not usually his "thing", but I knew it was worth publishing when the class cut-up laughed.

# Hullabaloo on Mainstreet

A satirical view of
America's bubble battles

# Table of Contents

# The Bagel Shop Bubble

The dawn wakens me with a crow from the rooster I hadn't had the heart to strangle this fall. I might be revising my opinion. I lay there savoring the slow march of light into the room. My wife Anabel and baby Jo are gone to visit Ana's parents in Arizona, so it's quiet except for the dog's nails on the living room's wood floor. I stare at the rustic beams supporting the roof for a few minutes, watching the weak November sun blush them with a pinkish hue as it filters through the mauve curtains.

It's time to get up. Here it is Wednesday and I really must settle down to write an article that's due tomorrow. I've procrastinated again, distracted by the solitude. I'd really rather spitball novel ideas than write about political philosophy. I'd justified the lack of focus. Yeah, the articles still paid the bills, but the novels were getting there. Maybe this one would move me from midlister to bestseller. Or not. Meanwhile, the mortgage is due every month and the articles pay the bills.

I pull on jeans and a fisherman's sweater to walk barefoot down the stairs to the living room. Beacon, our yellow Lab, perks up, jumps off the couch and stands at attention by the door. You really can't resent such conscience behavior. I let him out, toes curling as cold air flowed across them.

In the niche off the living room, my original research lies in neat piles around my laptop, but I have a lot of stream of consciousness sentences already on my zip drive. I've got to sit down and hammer them into an article today.

There's wood to chop and Beacon could use a bath and I promised Ana I'd paint the wall that separates the living room from my writing nook and the bathroom while she was gone. I could also work on the new bedroom up in loft. If Ana is pregnant again, I ... it's still an if and we'll have two years before we need the room.

Beacon barks, so I let him in. He climbs back up on his coach where he can look out the front windows at the distant cars on the road past our place. I ruffle his ears. He licks my hand. Does he wonder what I taste like or does he love me? He's a yellow Lab. Of course, he loves me! They don't actually taste their food.

Outside, it's a beautiful fall day. I wander to the fridge to look at the leftovers and the cheese. I finished the last of the fresh milk yesterday. I should have gone to the store, but I wrote a scene for the novel instead.

Fact is, nothing this side of the chicken coop screams "breakfast'" to me and maybe I've been a little isolated in the week I've been home alone. I can write that article anywhere. The research can be filled in later. Even a novelist can only spend so much time alone. I grab the laptop, ask Beacon if he wants to go for a ride, and we hop in the Jeep to head to town.

Fall is turning and winter is looming. The sun light's still golden but filtered through fewer leaves as I drive along the two-lane blacktop into town. The starkness of the sunlight says winter's right around the corner. The mostly-cleared fields still aren't frosted, but I give it another night, maybe until the weekend. The crispness to the air promises a turn toward winter is imminent. Beacon leans his chin on the window opening, tongue lolling in the breeze. How could he be four feet long and have a 12-foot-long tongue? I envision a hose reel at the back of his throat as a rope of drool splatters the side of my Jeep.

I pause at the corner of County Road R to allow a hay truck to cross. Tad Martin waves companionably. I salute him in return. Beacon sends his own greetings to Tad's Sheltie who is riding beside him. If the two were together, the Sheltie would come away soaked in drool. It's an hour past dawn and that hay truck is already full. I could never be a farmer. You have to wake up too early in the morning to capture the worm.

I love my hometown and am so grateful to have found my way back to it after more than a decade gone to the City. Like most little pockets of humanity where everybody knows everybody, there are quirks here that can rub you the wrong way sometimes, but I've learned to channel my sense of irritation and irrepressible irony into my writing, rather than challenge the people I use for source material. So far nobody has recognized themselves. Either they're not reading the books or it's a testament to my writing skills.

My favorite breakfast out is at The Bagel Emporium, right on Main Street, two blocks from City Hall and three blocks from my parents' hardware store. Either is a pleasant place to write when traffic is slow, but I start at the Emporium because bagels are more nutritious than nuts and bolts. I order a multi-grain with butter and a white-chocolate mocha breve in a cup that could double as a bathtub. While Shawn toasts my bagel and Pat makes my coffee, I settle down with my laptop at my favorite table with the etched-glass top and soda fountain chairs reupholstered in red and primary blue pleather. It nestles neatly into the sunny front window where Shawn has arranged all sorts of plants. It's like sitting in a garden when it's only 45 degrees outside. The weak November sun is just peeking over the buildings across the street, so that my little niche will soon be quite warm and bright.

I set up the article page and mute the Internet to limit its distractive power. The cursor blinks at me, insisting that something so innocent looking couldn't possibly be as ominous as I am casting it. Pat calls me to the counter.

"Oh, my god!" Her shriek immediately captures my attention as I accept my coffee bucket and bagel. Ellen Goodwin holds her tablet in front of her, horror contorting her features as the color drains from her face. I hadn't realized she has freckles. Is that black hair a dye job? "It's not possible!"

She taps frantically on the screen, muttering to herself, fingers twitching spasmodically. I exchange a glance with Pat, but it's his husband Shawn who answers my unspoken question.

"He won. Stole it right out from under her."

Stole what out from under whom? I've learned to parse my words and not take overt sides over the last few years. Oh, yeah, yesterday. The election might mean nothing to me beyond a current news event, but to some of my neighbors, the outcome is vital.

"Trump won the election?" I direct my question to Pat, who always seemed more reasonable than Shawn. Their marriage has that husband-and-wife vibe, a male-female ying-and-yang, Pat being the more cerebral and calm, Shawn the more emotional and effusive. Is that a gender-insensitive thought? My filter remains solid.

"It gets worse. He won this county by 27%."

Whoa! That's a lot. It doesn't really surprise me, but I'm hardly a good judge of an election. The polls had insisted Clinton would win, but trying to influence an election through demographic analysis is not the same as actually putting your finger on the pulse of the electorate. You just can't measure the depth and breadth of American political sentiment by asking 1000 people a question, no matter how well worded. The Trump signs in the yards had alerted me that our neighbors were planning to vote for him. Why are the bagel shop patrons surprised? Trump signs outnumbered Clinton signs by 4 to 1 as of last week. I wrote an article about it.

"I can't believe that a county that hasn't swung Republican in 45 years would vote in that pompous fascist." Shawn shakes his head sadly, eyes gleaming.

Why do you call people "Fascist"? They direct it at Trump, but others direct it at Clinton. The liberals called Bush a fascist and the conservatives called Obama a fascist. They can't all be fascists. Do you people even know what a fascist is? I've actually read Mussolini and I don't think you know what that word means. I have another word I'd use for both Clinton and Trump and it's not a really nice word. And, yes, it's only one word because I don't see a dime's worth of difference between the two.

"I can't believe Democrats would desert the party," Pat agrees. People apparently aren't allowed to notice the leftward march of the Democrat Party and to change their minds about their support. I'm pretty sure Republicans aren't allowed to notice the leftward march of the Republican Party and become libertarians either ... judging by how many Republicans now espouse traditional libertarian views.

"I thought I knew my neighbors." Ellen wipes a tear from her cheek, her voice quavering. She's actually crying

5

over an election result? Wow. Really? "I never realized they held such hatred in their hearts."

Hatred? Where'd that come from? What about Clinton's support of drone attacks? Syria? Yemen? That seems very hateful. I'm pretty sure if I were a Syrian or a Yemeni, I'd feel unloved after the missiles destroyed my home and blasted my family into small chunks of crispy-fried flesh. Not that I think Trump is a lovely human being. Nobody aspiring to higher office can be. They didn't get that far without hiding some bodies in a closet or five.

I return to my table and open my laptop to scan through the news. As a writer, the election is fodder for my imagination, though as a libertarian slouching toward anarchist, I hardly care personally. I hadn't cared enough to check the news feeds at home because I'm firmly of the opinion that neither candidate is worth getting excited about either way.

*Clowns to my right and crooks to my left ... here I am ... still not voting for you.*

"It's a mockery of the democratic process." It's not a huge building. I can easily see the counter and participate in the conversation. Shawn's round face bunches with tension, his reddish-gold eyebrows wriggling like wooly worms above his hazel eyes. Normally gentle, his eyes pulse with anger now. "She won the popular vote! It's a travesty. Why do they let those hicks make these stupid choices?"

Hicks? Uh, those are our neighbors you're talking about. That's just really rude. And, hey, I'm not a hick! I lived in the City for a decade. And you live here too ... hick!

"We've been here 15 years and tried to improve the schools and bring some thought into this community. It's as if all that time's been wasted." Pat shakes his head sadly.

Yeah, and that's the attitude they resent the most ... that you believe they need your guidance. Dad was talking about that last week, right after he rendered me speechless when he told me he was voting for Gary Johnson.

"The move-ins really need to learn to listen instead of talk. Your mom and I thought we were so smart when we got here, but we were all alone and we needed our neighbors' help to learn how to live out here in the middle of nowhere. You couldn't google how to split wood back then. By the time we felt brave enough to challenge some of the attitudes around here, the folks expressing them had started to make sense on a lot of issues. But the move-ins wouldn't know that because they're too busy telling other people what to think."

I don't want to brag, but I think that's my influence on my dad. Big head? Yeah, maybe. I've been a libertarian since senior year of high school and I've not shy about stating my philosophy to my family. When I first spouted forth, back before I learned discretion, my parents were typical statists ... bossy, opinionated, no appreciation of the non-aggression principle. Dad's come a long way in 15 years. So have I.

The bell over the door tinkles and Roberta Palmer enters with her customary box of pottery. While her big business is online, she sells some on consignment at local shops and does a brisk business most weeks. Today, her frizzy red hair is covered by a green beanie and her floral dress exposes black combat boots. She's covered the dress with a nubby purple sweater that would be loose on Jaba the Hut and could double as a 4-man tent on her bony frame. I love describing her outfits in my writing.

"Did you hear? I can't believe it! I passed Morgan Ratcliff on the corner and realized that it's now entirely possible that he might shoot me someday just because he can."

7

Don't spew, don't spew! Swallow! Relax your throat! Really, you must swallow if you want to breathe and the cream will be really hard to get off the screen. Swallow! There you go!

Are these people serious? Morgan is a big 2A guy who carries concealed often. Far as I know, he's never been angry about anything, much less shot anyone. A decade ago, his sister used a gun to scare a drunken man out of her house, and Morgan has been armed ever since. Okay, he was angry about that guy for about five minutes, just long enough to decide to go perma-concealed carry. Don't go uninvited into his house at night, Robbi darling. Don't rob the Gas-n-Sip and Morgan won't have any reason to pull his gun. I imagine Morgan laughing hysterically as I tell him what you just said. Stop being so over-dramatic! It's an election, not a post-apocalyptic movie!

"I've lived here for 12 years and I thought my neighbors were so polite and peaceful, but clearly, I have been misinterpreting them. They're all xenophobic sexists."

Xenophobic? All of them? The Baptist church raised $40,000 last year to settle a refugee family here. Lonan works at the feed store and Elspeth recently started a diaper service out of their garage. That's a lot of money for 150 xenophobes to raise to bring people they hate into the community.

Sexist? About half the businesses in town are owned by women and the female mayor won a third term with 62 percent of the vote two years ago. Maybe I have the wrong definition of sexist. It's possible. Are men allowed to define sexism? Maybe that's just one of those words pissed-off women get to shout when they're feeling particularly pissed off. Certainly men aren't allowed to point out the sexism of women. Women can't be sexist, we're told when we do.

"It must be a mistake." Ellen's eyes are still glued to the computer screen. It isn't a mistake. My news feed shows the reality. Trump has won 30 states and a clear majority of the electors. Clinton carried only the cities and a few liberal exurban counties on the coasts. I'd be apoplectic if I were a Democrat and dumbfounded if I were a Republican. As a libertarian, I think it probably doesn't matter which one won. "How could she win the popular vote and he win the Electoral College in a landslide? I'm sure they'll come out with a correction later today."

"This just goes to show why we need more of us on the school board and the Assembly."

How will that fix the Presidential election? Are you planning some sort of invasion of DC by teachers or ... er, uh, yeah? Hobby farmers unite against Trump! Real farmers unite against Hillary. Blood in the streets and UN blue helmets on the corners. Okay, now I'm being melodramatic, but at least I'm wise enough not to air my folly outside my head.

I know who Roberta means by "we". We are who the locals call "the move-ins". They ... er, we ... are all from somewhere else. They started filtering in slowly way back in the 1970s ... just a few artists and hobby farmers ... bringing their Avant Garde thinking and unusual fashion choices with them. My parents had been among the first ... young hipsters exhausted by the City, seeking the peace and tranquility of the country lanes and neat farm houses of Ford County. These days, coming up on 40 years of residency, they complain about the newer move-ins, the ones who mostly migrated here while I was gone to college and working in the City.

Joel Hackmuller comes in and stands by the cash register. He's a move-in too. I'm beginning to feel marginalized.

9

The locals long ago accepted my parents as fixtures. I suppose I am accepted as their son. The locals stopped asking Ana when we were planning to go "home" after the baby was born last year. She thinks that means we've become locals. I doubt it. We are still "they", but we have a hope of becoming locals, if we don't express our opinions too loudly for another decade or so.

I'd been off in the world when the pace of the migration picked up and surprised when I returned home for an extended visit ten years ago, to find a minority community of dread-locked artists and artisans growing up along the river. They weren't hippies taking a wrong turn on the way to dropping out like my parents had been. They had money and plans. They'd driven up property values and blocked access to the best fishing holes. By the time I moved back for real four years ago, they'd had kids and begun running for the county assembly and school board, advocating for substantive changes to the community ... changes the locals did not want. There'd been some heated Assembly meetings. Locals who previously hadn't cared much about politics had run for public office just to keep move-ins from winning.

"What are we going to do about this?" Trust Shawn to ask the pertinent questions. As if "we" could do anything about the outcome of a presidential election. Well, not me. I didn't vote and don't care ... mostly. But the entire Democratic party membership of Ford County doesn't amount to a drop in an ocean compared to the rest of the country. "We should launch an investigation into what sort of fraud occurred."

Fraud! My mom is a poll observer ... and as far as I know, still a Democrat. I can't imagine the paper ballots run through the scan counter could be manipulated, but okay, a recount would settle everybody's concerns ... as least until they realized that Trump won Ford County. Then they might all want to invest in some chamomile and kava before they pop arteries in their brains over the certain knowledge that they'll have to live with the "fraud" for four years.

Speak of the devil, in walks Bradly Morton, who won an east side Assembly seat by a whisker two years ago. Interesting that nobody suggested fraud that time because I suspected it. Either some locals hadn't voted or some ballots were stuffed. Bradley is just one of those guys you dislike instantly ... smooth as silk as he maneuvers you into things you don't want to do. They reiterate their questions as Pat makes Bradley's morning joe.

"The poll observers reported no irregularities. The hand counts of ballots matched the scanner counts. It appears she lost the election in this county without any help from voter fraud."

"But the popular vote …." Ellen isn't willing to let that one go.

Seriously? Are you that uneducated on the Constitution?

"The Electoral College allows for 51 state-wide elections." They all stare at me as if this is the first time I've ever spoken in my life. I am a political commentator, folks. I do this for a living. Remember? Byline in major publications …. This is what I do. "There is no national popular election. There are 51 statewide popular elections. Trump won 30 of them."

"There are only 50 states." Sniffing, Ellen rolls her eyes like I'm stupid.

"That includes Washington DC." I appreciate Bradley coming to my rescue, though I'm pretty sure we're not on the same side. Frankly, I don't want to be on the same side

11

as him. I like my odd little side ... my minority of one. "He won the Electoral College."

"But how is that possible if she won the popular vote?" Bradley defers to me now.

"The Electoral College is based on the number of Senators and Congressmen in a state, so it effectively allows weighted voting so that rural areas can have some say in who becomes president."

"When did that change?" Shawn's face is so red I worry he might have a stroke.

"1789. It's part of the original Constitution."

"But we elect presidents by the popular vote." Roberta's roots stand out starkly against her ashen skin. Is that a natural color or does she dye it? Wait, that was my thought about Ellen. Why am I suddenly obsessed with women's hair?

I can do political education while entertaining sarcastic thoughts. Or maybe it's because I can think sarcastic thoughts that I excel at political education. Humor makes it all so much less caustic and cruel.

"That's a media fiction. All presidents have always been selected by the Electoral College, although the statewide popular votes have been used to choose electors to the College since the 1840s."

They don't want to hear that. Facts just get in the way of their narrative. They start discussing how Trump will throw out the immigrants. Ellen won't be able to rely on Hector Hernandez to help her shear her sheep. I went to kindergarten with Hector and know his family. His father immigrated legally from Mexico. My parents attended his citizenship ceremony because Dad helped him study for the test. Hector was born a year later, so is not subject to deportation. Estrella Ortiz, an artist who sneaked in back in the 1990s and lives quietly, however …. I like Estrella. I hope ICE doesn't find her. I'm certainly not going to give them directions.

"What if Trump issues an executive order against marriage?" Shawn's crying now.

Did you not hear his convention speech? Trump seems quite comfortable with gay rights. When did my neighbors become snowflakes? Is there something wrong with me that my skin crawls when another man cries over an election result? I reserve tears for big events ... like my wedding and when my daughter was born. It's an election, for heaven sakes! He'll never get to govern in his own right. The Washington bureaucrats will soon tell him what's what and he'll fall in line or get shot in the head like Kennedy.

"I'm more afraid of our neighbors taking up pitchforks and surrounding our house."

Really, Pat? They didn't do that in the 12 years you were "partners". Yeah, there were people who refused to attend your wedding and only the Episcopalian church would host the ceremony, but exercising their right not to participate in a ceremony for a relationship they consider to be sin is not the same thing as being up in arms about the relationship. The only way the tar and features come out is if you start demanding they do things your way.

Of course, these are the things a polite person doesn't say in public, even in response to the most outrageous statements by ideologues. It pays to have a strong filter if you're an anarchist living in a community split between extreme liberals and solid conservatives. I'm starting to feel sympathy for my conservative neighbors. They are being misrepresented and they're not even here to defend themselves.

"I really thought we were finally reaching consensus with Obama's second election, but the Luddites just don't want to get along."

A brief image of Bradley pulling the strings for puppet neighbors pops into my head. Don't spew! Breathe!

"The economy was finally recovering after all of Obama's hard work and now they're going to turn back to Reaganomics and it'll all go to hell again."

Joel's simplistic understanding of economics would probably make me snort if I wasn't afraid it would result in stoning with day-old bagels followed by a mocha water-boarding.

My coffee cup is just about empty, so I drain it and take the cup to the bus bucket. Ellen brightens.

Oh, oh! What do you want? My more liberal neighbors have no problem asking for help. Tad Martin, one of the most conservative men in the county, could be trapped under his hay wagon and if you asked him if he needed help, he'd reply "Well, if you've got some time and it wouldn't be too much trouble, I'd be grateful if you'd get this thing off me. Otherwise, if you're busy, could you call my wife and let her know I need a hand here? You know, when you've got the time." But our liberals hereabout have a great deal more self-esteem than the conservatives. They just come right out and ask you to sweat for them.

"I'm supposed to go meet Gil Wanaker at my barn to receive a load of hay. Connor, would you come with me? I just don't feel safe with him right now."

Really? Gil Wanaker, Baptist deacon, farmer, crafter of the most beautiful wood furniture to grace a home or business -- *that* Gil Wanaker? He adopts squirrels (of the nut-gathering variety) and is on the volunteer fire department. I have an article to write, but I'm intrigued by this source of material in my neighbors, so I agree and hop in my Jeep to follow her in her Prius. The morning has thoroughly developed into a crisp golden day. I wonder how often she has to replace her shocks driving this rough gravel road. Gil's old red Power Wagon is just coming around the bend from the other direction when we pull into her driveway and park to the side of the barn.

This was the Phillips Farm before both their kids went to college in the City and never came back except to visit. The Phillips now live in town in a small house surrounded by an enormous truck garden. They still sell some wonderful vegetables at the Farmer's Market. Happily nested in the huge house that sheltered three generations of Phillipses, Ellen now raises goats and sheep and makes artisan cheeses, which she sells to restaurants in the City. She also runs a bed & breakfast since she has a lot of room.

"Morning, Connor. Being a good neighbor, I see." Gil wears a red watch cap against the November chill. His bright blue eyes twinkle merrily, but there are lines around them that suggest he holds thoughts about Ellen right now that I wish I knew. He steps up on the tire to unhook the straps and fold back the tarp. "Ellen, you want to inspect the hay?"

Everybody knows that Gil gives full measure, always, but it's nearly 9:30 and the truck bed isn't full. Anders Randolph, the most voracious Bernie Sanders supporter I'd ever met, lives in the direction Gil just came from. Did he ask you to inspect the hay? That's so carrying politics too far.

Ellen starts guiltily and shoots me a look. What? Do you think I can project my thoughts into his head? Talk to your neighbor. Seriously, all this fear of one another and misunderstanding points of view could be cleared up if people would just talk to one another. You're still the same people you were yesterday. You just disagree on an election result. It's just a popularity contest, not something important like God or what to name the dog.

"Of course not, Gil. Let me show you where I want it."

Afraid to make him angry? What have we come to all because of an election between two terribly flawed candidates? Neighbor can't talk to neighbor. Is it just our little backwater or as the whole nation gone around the bend without a paddle? I vote for the whole nation. We're really that schizophrenic these days.

With me there, Ellen doesn't really need to help with unloading the hay. It would look a little silly for me to stand there doing nothing. Gil suggests she go warm up and we get to work unloading the hay together. I've volunteered like this before because I like exploring ordinary lives. It makes good articles and novels.

"Why are you here, really?"

Gil might be a conservative, but he is also a very reasonable man who doesn't need me to filter my thoughts, so I opt for honest. It feels refreshing.

"All the move-ins are freaking out that Trump won and Ellen suspects you voted for him."

"What was her first clue? My Trump bumper sticker?" We laugh together. "That still doesn't explain why you're here."

"She's not the only one who is afraid of their Trump-voting neighbors this morning."

"Oh, for heaven's sake! Are they expecting us to suddenly launch Kristal Nacht here in the Midwest?"

Oh, that line is so going in the article! That is not a hick reference. This man reads, maybe more than his condescending neighbors.

"Can I ask … why did you vote for him?"

His face contorts slightly as we heft the first bale of hay and carry it into the barn.

"You know how my kid just bought McCormick's Drug Store?"

Frank had lived in the City for nearly 20 years. He just returned this summer, bought an empty store that had once been a thriving business and set up a bakery.

"He owned a bakery in the City. Great business until he turned down making a fully decorated wedding cake for a lesbian couple."

Oh! Of course! I'd read about it and didn't connect the last names.

"The government said he had to pay a hundred thousand in fines and go to reeducation courses … make his employees go to these psychological manipulation classes. He couldn't do it. He sold the business, paid the fines and moved here, across the stateline so they can't follow him. He'll never bake another wedding cake and if you've noticed an improvement in the bagels at Pat & Shawn's, you can see that he's not opposed to doing business with gays, just to catering their weddings."

I feel for Frank because I'd refuse to decorate the cake too. Other people's lifestyles are none of my business, but when they demand I participate, I will demand the right to refuse. I don't go to second weddings of church members either. It's my personal choice. If you ask me why, I'll tell you, but I don't expect anyone to do it with me.

We return to the truck to get another bale. A squirrel chitters and throws pinecone pieces at us as we heft down the next one.

"Hillary was for making those pushy rules even stronger, turning this country into a place where people of faith are forced to violate their beliefs on a regular basis and are only allowed to exercise their values inside the walls of the church. I just couldn't vote for that."

After we set the bale down, I pause to read a text from my mother.

"I mostly agree with you on that, Gil. I didn't vote either way, but I gotta ask … what about the misogyny and racism?"

"I don't agree with the locker room talk, but he's no worse than Bill Clinton was. I also don't hire illegals to work on my farm. I hire teenagers at minimum wage. It costs me more money and I can't pocket the taxes like some do, but it's against the law to hire illegals or to pay Americans less than minimum wage. Until we do away with entitlements, it's just not fair that people who can work outside the law can come here and take jobs from Americans for what they're actually worth and then qualify for entitlements that Americans paid for."

He sounds so reasonable that I have to mostly agree with him. A welfare state and open borders is a recipe for crushing taxation. While I like immigrants, I don't like taxes.

# The Hardware Store Bubble

After the hay is unloaded, I head back into town where my parents are hosting an impromptu gathering in the hardware store. It had been Dad's nostalgic idea to have a woodstove with chairs around it so people could gather, drink coffee, and shoot the breeze. They probably sell a bit more hardware because of it, but mostly it's a social gathering. Over the years, it has become a Saturday staple for the locals. It's rare to see a move-in. They'd be welcome, but they self-segregate by driving to the box store two towns over. What they save on widgets, they shell out in gas. On this midweek midday, the locals plunk down 50 cents for their coffee and a dollar or two for a baked good and hold forth on the way the move-ins are acting. It's a mixture of celebratory laughter and annoyance.

"My god, you'd think we'd elected Hitler."

I don't think Trump is Hitler. Der Furor was a scary man with no sense of humor. Trump is more like Bozo the clown.

"Hillary is the fascist. She'd take away the guns and force us all to bow to the government."

There's that term "fascist" again. If I had to measure Hillary and Trump for the sash reading "authoritarian dictator" … uh, a dead-heat. I give her points for shrill. I'll give him points for inconsistent. She gets some points for actually doing some authoritarian activities while in government. He gets some points for espousing some authoritarian ideas while campaigning. Still a dead-heat.

"Our taxes would go up."

Trump's talking stimulus and not even mentioning the debt. Government can't grow without increasing taxes because we're at unsustainable levels of debt, guys. Of course, most of the folks in the hardware store want to reduce the size of government … well, the parts they don't like, anyway. They're big on growing the military and farm subsidies.

"Our kids would have to march off to her wars."

Oh, yeah! You people have no idea how many wars that woman started or enlarged while she was Secretary of State! Well, yeah, you have the Internet too. And, wait a minute, aren't you the patriots who encourage your kids to join the military? It's okay for them to join the military, but not to go to war? I thought the purpose of the military was to go to war. Or is it just the wars liberals start that you disagree with?

The bagel shop must have had an early run on lunches because most people have bags bearing the logo. Some who came from the west side of town have bags with Speedy Sub Shop's logo. Mom must have asked Frank to bring baked goods because he's leaning against the oil-rubbed-patinaed counter next to a huge basket that probably cleaned out his inventory. The beauty of the small town entrepreneur was you can close if you sell out your inventory. I really must interview him for an article.

"Trump's going to rebuild our military and prevent more wars."

Really? Does the largest military in the world really need rebuilding? Do we have to have troops in the Netherlands? Couldn't we stop spreading our strength over hundreds of countries?

"He's going to build that wall, stop the invasion."

I had lived for a while in Phoenix and know that the "invasion" is real. My father-in-law is a border rancher who has lost tens of thousands of dollars in property damage and theft when groups of migrants come through. That's an invasion, but the illegals who milk the cows at the corporate dairies here live quietly and spend their money locally … well, what they don't send home to Mexico to enable more of their family and friends to join them here in the Land of Milk and Honey and ever-flowing government benefits. I'm a wall-skeptic. There are some impressive fences along parts of the border and the cartels just dig tunnels under them.

"He's going to get rid of Obamacare."

Hear-hear! Why is a perfectly healthy 34-year-old man forced to pay for medical insurance he has no reason to use? Until this year, Anabel and I had carried a catastrophic policy and a bank account. We'd paid cash for our pregnancy and delivery, using a direct midwife, which had cost less than the deductible on a standard medical insurance policy. When I'd finally looked into getting full medical insurance this year to avoid the tax consequences, I'd been shocked at the price. Bye-bye bank account! If one of us gets sick, we'll have to go into debt to pay our portion. I'd rather have a bank account. Is the point of insurance now to make medical care unaffordable?

The gathering of two dozen people is about evenly split between men and women. Some of these women own businesses. Did they just not notice that Trump is a misogynist who would see them in the kitchen, barefoot and pregnant?

"I hope he tightens the entries from the Middle East and Europe." Hector is standing on the other side of the woodstove, but hearing him speak, I remember that his brother was severely wounded in a terrorist attack in France. I'd done a column on it. "We need to tighten the refugee standards, make sure they're not terrorists before they come into the country, not wait for them to shoot up a mall."

How immigration screeners can suss out if someone will become a terrorist 10 years from now isn't clear to me, maybe because I'm trying to figure how these racist nationalists seem unaware that Hector is Hispanic? Is he unaware that they're racist nationalists? Why isn't he over at the bagel shop with the touchy-feeling people who want to keep him from being deported?

"Gun-free zones … free fire zones … people disarmed for the convenience of crazies."

I'm personally in favor of shooting back. I ignore those "gun-free zone" signs at the mall too. I pour myself a cup of coffee and select a bun. It's close enough to lunch. I drop money into the pay bowl.

"After eight years of Obama running this country into the ground, not listening to the people who built this country, maybe the liberals will finally learn what it feels like."

Whoa! It's like a giant tug of war. One president represents one side and the next president represents the other. And as they tug back and forth, one side or the other finally has their chance to be heard … until the rope breaks and spills them all on their butts in the mud.

Are our neighbors right about the Trump voters, after all? Here's my chance to find out.

"I'm doing research for an article. So, can I ask a few questions?"

They all agree or don't object, which amounts to the same thing. Everybody likes the idea of being in an article, especially in a national publication.

"How many of you were Democrats before this election?"

Fifty percent. A few of the other half offer that they were Democrats until just a few years ago. That brings the total to about 80% former Democrats. This county's been Democrat-majority since the Depression. What would cause them to change their political identity?

"How many of you voted for Obama the first time?" Surprisingly, only Hector didn't. Why didn't you vote for the black president, *amigo*? Are you a closet racist? "How many of you voted for Obama the second time?" Out of 25 people, 10 had. "Why didn't you vote for him the second time?"

"The economy ... his pushy social agenda ... drone attacks ... killing an American citizen without due process ... Obamacare ... al-Alwaki ... gun running into Mexico against gun shop owners objections ... Obamacare ... the militarization of the police ... Obamacare ...."

"Why didn't you vote for Hillary?"

"Benghazi ... Wikileaks ... comments denigrating country folk ... Obamacare started as Hillarycare ... wars ... arrogance ... Obamacare ... I read the emails ... deplorables ... no understanding of business ... Obamacare ...."

"What would you like the move-ins to do? Now that the Republicans are in complete charge of 18 states and partially of five others and all branches of the federal government ... what would you like to hear from the move-ins?"

They actually think about it. I'm proud of the conservative part of my community.

"Nothing." It's my dad, making more coffee while my mom empties the pay bowl. "If I could control other people to do what I wanted, I'd want them to sit quietly for a year and not say anything."

Really? I envision the bagel shop coterie tied to chairs with duct tape over their mouths, sitting here amidst their neighbors. It's a brilliant idea. My parents would spend the rest of their lives in prison for kidnapping, but it might be worth it.

"We were move-ins once too." Mom addresses the whole group, who are already nodding to what Dad said. I sometimes wonder how my long lankiness came out of this neat pocket-sized woman with her fading blond pixie cut and Harry Potter glasses. "The opinions here were so odd to hear, coming from where we were coming from. But we were nervous to argue with anyone, so we didn't and pretty soon, we realized that the people here are kind and thoughtful and we began to agree with what some of you were saying."

Proud of my parents! Proud of the other people here too because they laugh. You were all so welcoming once. Did you change or did the quality of move-ins degrade?

"They don't talk with us." Jill Ilene nods her head, setting her graying curls bouncing. "If they'd talk with us, they'd know we just want our country back."

"Demographics are changing." I'm still playing reporter. "The country is changing with it."

"If we stopped the invasion of migrants, Americans wouldn't become the minority in their own country." Roger Palshaw has his feet propped up by the stove, his big hands hooked in his red suspenders. My age, he inherited the farm from his parents who are now enjoying raising his kids while his wife runs a fabric store in town. "We'd have time to assimilate the folks who are already here."

Hector's nodding. I suppose my parents played a role in assimilating his parents. Nobody held a gun to their heads. They wanted to become Americans.

"I'd like them to stop running for the school board, stop trying to indoctrinate our kids with their leftist lunacy." Also my age, Marian George sold her parents' farm and opened a floral shop. She and Drew have five children that his mother home-schools to avoid the leftist lunacy. Marian provided some beautiful floral arrangements when Shawn and Pat got married last year. I didn't attend the ceremony, but I've seen the photos framed on the bagel shop walls as if trying to rub their neighbor's noses in it.

"I'd like them to listen to why we believe as we do." Pastor Newton leans against one of the nail bins. "They never listen. They just talk at us and expect us to 'learn' from them. They assume we couldn't teach them anything worthwhile?"

Beside my family, you're the only college-educated person in this room, Pastor. The move-ins consider the rest of them ignorant hicks. Fact is, I know what Pastor Newton means. It's frustrating to talk to the move-ins because they are so certain they are right, so certain they are smarter than the rest of us. I get a few points for having gone to college, but I lose IQ points in their estimation just because I was born here and came back. Einstein would have been a dunce to the move-ins.

"I'd like them to stop destroying businesses because the owners hold beliefs that aren't popular this decade." Frank's comment is quietly stated. I smile at Frank to assure him I'm on his side. Like most people who have been through a long period of statist abuse, he's still having trouble meeting gazes.

"So, what if Trump is really the disaster they think he's going to be? What if his policies tank the economy, start wars all over the world and alienate our allies?"

They frown, but Roger laughs a second later.

"Let it burn." That prompts some concerned expressions, but he continues. "If this country keeps on the same way it's been going under Obama, there'd be nothing to pick up anyway. That's why I voted against Hillary. I think Trump might screw it up, but I think he's less likely to start rounding up regular folks because he recognizes that it'll be folks like us who pick up the pieces. Fancy cheeses and weird paintings are not what's going to rebuild the country. It's men and women who know how to do something useful that'll be needed."

My god! The head of the local RNC, Roger sounds almost like a libertarian anarchist. Color me shocked! He hasn't just been arguing his views when we meet over beers. He's actually been listening. Dogs will be mating with cats any moment now. In fact, I should make sure Beacon isn't being molested by Mom's cat as we speak.

"That means some rough times for all of us. What happens to people who … let's say … write articles and books for a living … during those hard times?"

"Nothing wrong with writing articles. We need reporters. We used to have a daily here. And at least you're balanced. You bashed both Trump and Clinton in your articles."

Yes, I am an equal opportunity basher. If you're a politician, I don't love you. Hope my siblings or parents don't decide to run for office. I'll bash them too, which might make Thanksgiving awkward.

"But long as you get busy doing useful things like reporting real news, there's no reason you should starve." Pastor Newton's sermons are always tinged with humor and he winks at me now.

"But the move-ins would be forced to face reality … find they're not in control just because they went to college and lived in the big City." Roger looked so comfortable, sitting there. I hope Trump doesn't disappoint him too much.

"Besides, I don't think Trump is going to fix the country without our help." Morgan Ratcliff says. "If we want liberty, we're going to have to fight for it and impose the necessary conditions on those who would oppose it."

Yeah, he's quoting something, but Morgan also reads, a lot, so he might understand what he's just said, which is that he's in favor of forcing his neighbors, as they tried to force him, to do it his way. But what if that isn't my way … or Roger's way? I believe people can best run their own lives. It's fantasy land to think that someone you've never met can best run the lives of others.

"You're looking thoughtful, son." Pastor Newton stares at me. "What's on your mind?"

"Democracy is the act of periodically choosing who will be master and who will be slave. I don't vote because I can't rightfully talk myself into forcing other people into living my way."

"We're not forcing anyone. Voting doesn't force anyone." Drew's a minarchist; I suspect Marian has had this conversation before. I don't throw her husband under the bus.

"Doesn't it? Seems to me that for eight years you folks were forced to see cherished principles degraded and rights curtailed under the Obama administration. A lot of those values are my values too, so I know how it felt. Now, for the next four to eight years, you want to force the other side to do things your way. That's what voting does. It decides that some people can push other people around based on the outcome of a popularity contest."

"Well, the alternative is shooting at one another." Morgan might be at all times armed, but he is a gentle soul who doesn't want to kill anyone unless forced to do it by their behavior. He'd rather just use the government's force.

"No, the alternative is talking to one another and working it out."

"Yeah, but they don't listen." Marian points toward the bagel shop.

Do you? My filter is solid. It won't let me say that, though I hope some of them think it. I hope Drew says it to her. Pastor Newton has a thoughtful look on his face.

"You might be right, son, that we need to listen too," he agrees.

"So, let me ask you a question." Roger still hasn't moved. Maybe he's grown roots in that chair, which will complicate janitorial for my parents. "You don't vote, but you have an idea of how the world would be ideal." I nod. "So, how do you expect that to come about? I mean, the modern world decides things by election, son, and anarchists don't vote. Your ideal's not coming about through an election because won't you always be outvoted by even one person when it comes to deciding things?"

He has a point. It's on the back of his head right above his brainstem. I've often struggled with this concept too. If you're a committed democrat, it sucks when your side loses the election. If you're a committed anarchist, you never win the election because you can't even vote for yourself.

But they're thinking, so maybe something good will come of this wasted morning. I announce I'd better head home to write my article and go out to the Jeep on the street. While Beacon relieves his bladder with a leg raised to a telephone pole, I envision Main Street as a vast canyon between two irreconcilable ideologies which exist in their separate bubbles.

Anabel and the kid won't be home for another week, so I decide to stop by the bagel shop one last time to buy a few days' worth of breakfast because after I finish writing this article, I'm going to want a break from discussing politics and I really don't think that's going to happen at the Bagel Emporium.

It's lunch now, so there are different people here freaking out about the same thing. While Shawn wrangles my bagels into a bag, I listen to Cheryl Langdon talk about how abortions will soon be illegal in the United States and how women will be dying in the streets then. Tad Martin, a committed pro-life advocate with four kids he's delivered himself with midwife supervision, looks uncomfortable eating his sandwich while she talks over his head in that fake preachy voice she dons. She not really talking to Melani Wright who is a member of the same ideology. She's aiming her remarks at Tad and he knows it.

Roberta pops back into the shop to order lunch. There's clay under her fingernails. Tad puts his plate and cup in the bus bin and then stops behind me to speak to her.

"My bride's birthday is in two weeks. I've been wondering if I can buy one of your pots for her."

Tad's been married to Arlinda for at least 15 years, since the weekend after high school graduation. I think it's kind of cute that he calls her "my bride". I'm going to have to try that on Ana. She'll see through my mechanizations, I'm sure.

"Of course you can," Roberta replies. "Do you want something custom or one already made?"

"Her favorite color is turquoise and she's been keeping her potpourri in a basket on the hearth, but the kids landed on it wrestling the other day. So, I thought she might want something to replace it."

"So, something kind of shallow and wide. You know, I have a teal pot that you might like. It's sort of custom because it was a happy mistake when the glaze turned out wrong. Teal is close to turquoise."

"She likes teal too. It was one of the colors at our wedding and it'll match the duck decoy on the mantle."

Roberta grins at that word picture.

"Drop by my shop after 3 today and I'll show it to you. If that doesn't suit you, I can design something. I have a kiln run going next week and I could throw a special pot before then."

"I'll do that. Thanks, Miss Robbi."

Roberta has her notebook out, sketching. She shows it to him.

"Yeah, that's exactly what I'm looking for. I'll be there this afternoon."

He smiles and nods and she smiles back. As he heads out the door, they exchange waves like they're best friends.

Therein lays the irony. The town's liberals and conservatives need one another, so they'll continue doing business together, even while being suspicious of each other's motives and fearful of sanctions. Between bouts of panicking on social media, they will continue buying and selling and getting along in the market where all exchanges are voluntary ... and completely miss that freedom exists there and that opportunity stems from freedom. They'll squabble over this election result for four years and never realize all the energy being wasted that could be turned to something more useful ... like watching paint dry or grass grow ... or staring at me trying to write a column when I haven't been inspired by current events.

There will be no paint drying while I write today. I head home to set the keyboard afire.

### Breakwater Harbor Books

Fantasy, science fiction, crime thriller, psychological fiction, Christian, wasabi punk, romance, women's fiction, poetry, political satire ... and more.

breakwaterharborbooks.com

# Other Books by Lela Markham

# About Lela Markham

Hi. I was raised in a house made of books in Alaska and told tales from the time I could talk. A teacher eventually made me write one of them down. I hated the exercise, but it was the spark that ignited a fire that has never gone out.

My daring husband, two fearless offspring and I live the adventure of a lifetime here on the Last Frontier where the midnight sun encourages wandering the wilderness and the long dark winters favor reading, writing and staring at the northern lights … hence the moniker Aurorawatcher.

It's all about the aurora watching!

# Give an Author a Hand!
# Leave a Review on Amazon or another fine retailer!

www.ingramcontent.com/pod-product-compliance
Lightning Source LLC
Chambersburg PA
CBHW032113170626
46808CB00008B/3046